ACROSS THE SEA

PaRragon

Bath • New York • Cologne • Melbourne • Delhi
Hong Kong • Shenzhen • Singapcre • Amsterdam

This edition published by Parragon Books Ltd in 2015

Parragon Books Ltd
Chartist House
15–17 Trim Street
Bath BA1 1HA, UK
www.parragon.com

ISBN 978-1-4748-1091-3

Printed in China

From the movie

Disney FROZEN

ACROSS THE SEA

"There's our ship, Elsa!" Anna exclaimed, peering out of the window. "Are you almost ready?"

"Just about," Elsa replied as she packed the last of her things. She smiled at her sister's impatience, but really, she couldn't wait to go either.

Elsa had been planning a Royal Tour to visit nearby kingdoms for a few months. And now it was time to leave! Her heart fluttered with anxious excitement.

As soon as the sisters climbed aboard their ship, the captain scurried over. "Your Majesty," he said to Elsa. "I have the itinerary you sent. But I don't think we'll make it to the first stop on time. Not with waters this still."

"Don't worry," Anna said, taking the wheel.

"We've got it covered," Elsa said, smiling. "I'll give us a little nudge."
She raised her arms and created a light snow flurry, pushing the ship
along at a steady pace.

"Woo-hoo!" Anna cried from her post, the flurry blowing through
her hair. "Away we go!"

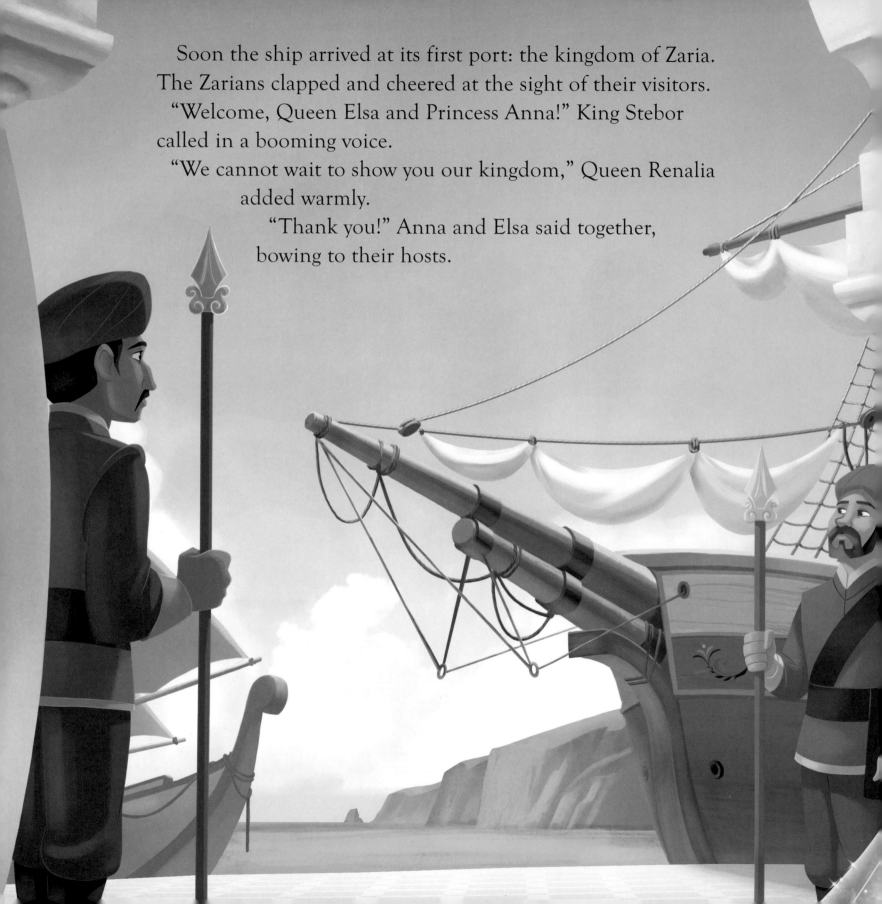

Soon the ship arrived at its first port: the kingdom of Zaria.
The Zarians clapped and cheered at the sight of their visitors.
"Welcome, Queen Elsa and Princess Anna!" King Stebor
called in a booming voice.
"We cannot wait to show you our kingdom," Queen Renalia
added warmly.
"Thank you!" Anna and Elsa said together,
bowing to their hosts.

First, the king and queen of Zaria invited the sisters to lunch, where Anna and Elsa enjoyed lively conversation and tasty food they had never tried before.

"Renalia thought I couldn't talk when we first met. I was so nervous around her," King Stebor told them.

"Oh, that's sweet!" Anna said.

"Yes, except now he won't stop talking," Queen Renalia joked playfully.

Then Anna and Elsa were taken on a tour of Zaria's prized gardens, where there were many colourful and sweet-smelling blossoms and shrubs on display.

Elsa pointed out a flower that looked remarkably like their friend, Olaf.

"We'll be sure to send you home with some of those seeds, then," King Stebor said.

That night, they were treated to a grand festival.

"We've heard so much about your special talents," Queen Renalia said to Elsa. "Won't you show us some of your magic?"

Suddenly, Elsa felt very shy. She gave a little icy flourish with her hands and then looked at the floor.

"Would you like to join the dancing, Your Majesties?" she asked, changing the subject. "That looks like fun."

The king and queen agreed and the rest of the evening was filled with music and fun.

The next stop on Anna and Elsa's tour was a kingdom called Chatho. The sisters met Chatho's ruler, Queen Colisa, in front of her impressive palace.

"Thank you for having us, Your Majesty," Elsa said.

"Of course," the queen responded. "I am very happy you are both here!"

Queen Colisa first took the sisters on a walk through the
kingdom's rainforest, where they saw many unique animals.
Anna was fond of some particularly bashful furry creatures.
"Why, hello there!" she cooed.

Next, the queen led Anna and Elsa into an enormous gallery. Chatho was known for its striking art and relics.

"These are beautiful," Elsa said.

"I'm so glad you think so," Queen Colisa replied. "Would you like to add a sculpture to our collection?"

Suddenly, Elsa noticed a block of
ice under a spotlight, ready to be carved.
Once again, she felt a wave of shyness.
    Noticing her sister's discomfort, Anna jumped in.
"Um ... sure! Ice sculptures are actually my speciality!"

Later, Anna gently asked Elsa why she didn't want to show her powers.

"I guess I just got nervous," Elsa admitted.

Anna smiled. "Well that's silly. You can do wonderful things." She grabbed some of the snow that had been created by Elsa's magic and placed it on her upper lip. "You can even give me a new look!"

Elsa laughed and hugged her sister. "Thanks, Anna. You're ..."

"... the Duke of Weselton!" The sisters had arrived at their next port, only to see a familiar face. This duke had been very unkind to Elsa when her icy gifts were first revealed.

"What are you doing here?" Anna asked. The sisters had purposefully avoided Weselton on their tour. Their last stop was the kingdom of Mandonia, far from Weselton.

The Duke smoothed his coat as Anna and Elsa got off the ship. "I am visiting my mother's cousin's wife's nephew if you must know. Although I wish I hadn't. If I were you, I would turn your ship round right now."

The sisters looked at one another.

The Duke sighed, clearly exasperated. "Mandonia has had the hottest summer in years. It is just unbearable! Of course, you wouldn't care about that."

"Take us to the kingdom," Elsa said firmly to the harrumphing duke. Anna grinned and put her arm through her sister's.

As the Duke led the sisters into the village, they felt as though they were stepping into a hot, sticky cloud. The Maldonians were sprawled out, sweaty and tired.

"Whoa," Anna remarked.

Elsa didn't feel one bit shy. She knew she had to help these people cool down. After conjuring some snow clouds, Elsa saw the townspeople start to come to life.

"It's working," the Duke cried in surprise.

"Why don't you get us some lemonade?" Elsa prompted the Duke.

She started making some frosted mugs out of ice.

"Thank you, Queen Elsa. Thank you!" the crowd cheered.

Soon, Mandonia became a frozen wonderland. The citizens
even had enough energy to slide down the new snowy piles on
wooden planks. Anna grabbed one for Elsa.

"I suppose a thank you is in order," the Duke said begrudgingly.
"I frankly don't know where to begin...."

"Well, you could grab a board," Elsa suggested, winking at Anna.

The Duke turned red and started spluttering. "Well ... a duke would
never ... it isn't ..."

"It's okay. We'll show you how it's done," Anna called, racing her sister
up the hill and back down again.

A few hours later, it was time for Anna and Elsa to return to Arendelle.
They waved to their new friends from the ship.

"Did you have a good trip?" Anna asked her sister.

"I did," Elsa replied as she created a blast of icy snow to direct them homeward.
"I'd say that was the best Royal Tour ever ... until next time, that is!"

The End